My "m" Sound Box®

Library of Congress Cataloging-in-Publication Data
Moncure, Jane Belk.
My "m" sound box / by Jane Belk Moncure; illustrated by Colin King.
p. cm.
Summary: A little boy fills his sound box with many words that begin with the letter "m."
ISBN 1-56766-779-1 (lib. bdg. : alk. paper)
[1. Alphabet.] I. King, Colin, ill. II. Title.
PZ7.M739 Mym   2000
[E]—dc21   99-055421

My "m" Sound Box®

Jane Belk Moncure

illustrated by Colin King

The Child's World®

Little  had a box.

"I will find things that begin
with my 'm' sound," he said.

"I will put them into my sound box."

Little m found monkeys.

Did he put the monkeys into his box? He did.

Then Little  found a mouse.

Then he found another  mouse,

and another  mouse.

He found many mice!

Did he put the mice into the box with the monkeys? He did.

But the monkeys did not like the mice.

The monkeys were mad!

They jumped out of the box

and ran . . .

up a mountain.

Little  ran up the mountain.

The mice ran up the mountain, too.

Then the monkeys ran down the mountain.

The monkeys were so mad,
they did not see

the mud!

The monkeys fell into the mud!

Now they were very mad.

What a mess!

Little  and the mice pulled the monkeys out of the mud.

The monkeys were still mad.

Little  put the monkeys
back into the box.

"Mice, be nice!" he said.

"I must find something else for my mice."

Just then,

Little  met a

moose.

"Moose," he said, "you are just what I need for my mice."

Little 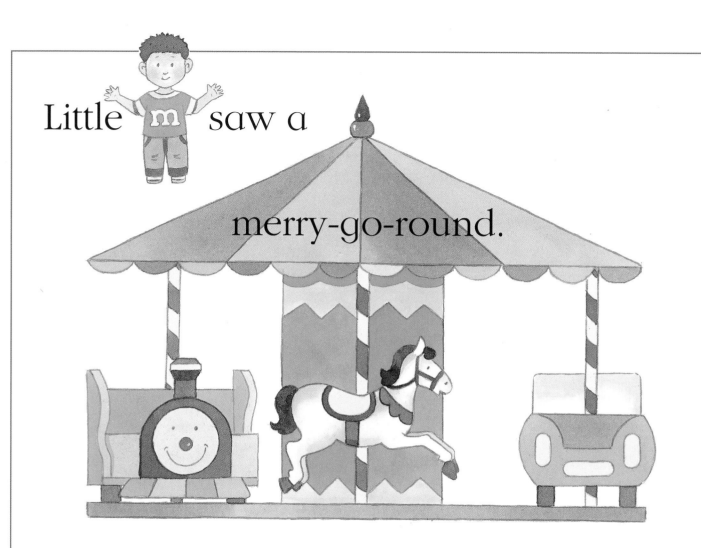 saw a merry-go-round.

"Let's ride the merry-go-round," he said.

He found some money.

And they all went for a ride on
the merry-go-round.

Then Little  looked up
and saw the moon.

"The moon belongs in my box!"
he said. "How can I get the moon?"

Just then,

Little  met a magician.

"The moon is too big
for your box," said the magician.

"But I will take you to the moon in my

magic moon machine."

And he did!

He took them all the way to the moon.

Some magic!

monkey

mouse

moose

moon

magician

mouse

magic moon machine

mouse

monkey

mouse

monkey

27

Can you read these words with Little 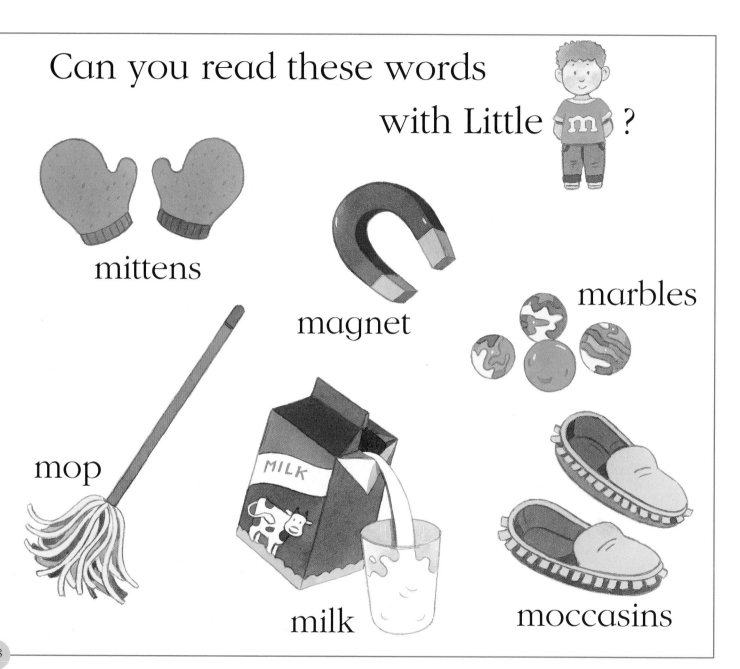 ?

mittens

magnet

marbles

mop

milk

moccasins

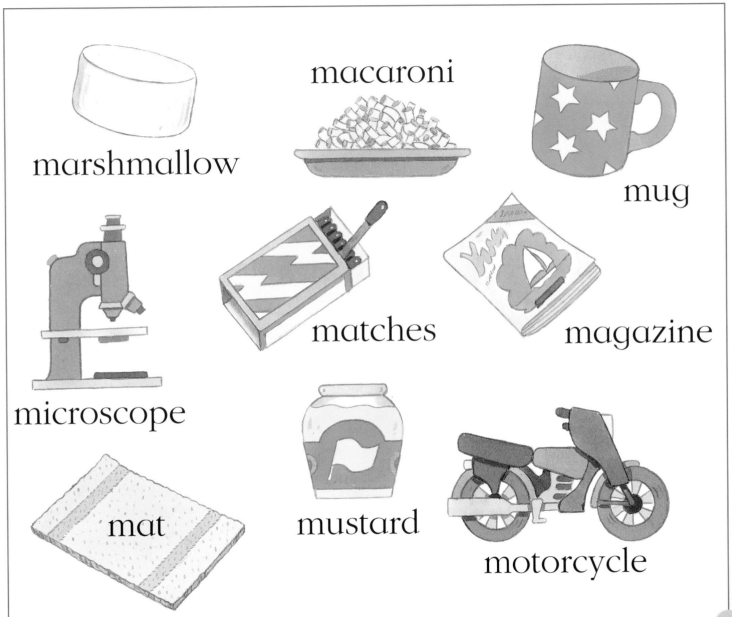

marshmallow

macaroni

mug

microscope

matches

magazine

mat

mustard

motorcycle

29

ABOUT THE AUTHOR AND ILLUSTRATOR

Jane Belk Moncure began her writing career when she was in kindergarten. She has never stopped writing. Many of her children's stories and poems have been published, to the delight of young readers, including her son Jim, whose childhood experiences found their way into many of her books.

Mrs. Moncure's writing is based upon an active career in early childhood education. A recipient of an M.A. degree from Columbia University, Mrs. Moncure has taught and directed nursery, kindergarten, and primary grade programs in California, New York, Virginia, and North Carolina. As a former member of the faculties of Virginia Commonwealth University and the University of Richmond, she taught prospective teachers in early childhood education.

Mrs. Moncure has travelled extensively abroad, studying early childhood programs in the United Kingdom, The Netherlands, and Switzerland. She was the first president of the Virginia Association for Early Childhood Education and received its award for outstanding service to young children.

A resident of North Carolina, Mrs. Moncure is currently a full-time writer and educational consultant. She is married to Dr. James A. Moncure, former vice president of Elon College.

Colin King studied at the Royal College of Art, London. He started his freelance career as an illustrator, working for magazines and advertising agencies.

He began drawing pictures for children's books in 1976 and has illustrated over sixty titles to date.

Included in a wide variety of subjects are a best-selling children's encyclopedia and books about spies and detectives.

His books have been translated into several languages, including Japanese and Hebrew. He has four grown-up children and lives in Suffolk, England, with his wife, three dogs, and a cat.